P9-EDP-974

Contents

Homerun Hitter

Jo Ann Yolanda Hernández

SCHOLASTIC INC.

New York   Toronto   London   Auckland   Sydney
Mexico City   New Delhi   Hong Kong

**Cover illustration by
John Ward**

**Interior illustrations by
W.C. Carani**

1 The Game

"Just one more chance," Carmen Durán whispers to herself. "Please, let me get one more chance at bat."

It's the last inning, and Carmen's team, the Cougars, are up. But they're behind by three runs. And they have two outs.

In the dugout, Carmen holds her favorite bat and watches the game.

She can hear her parents yelling and cheering. Carmen is kind of embarrassed, but deep inside she's glad they are here. Her dad is okay. He never mentions the times she drops the ball or strikes out.

Across the field, she sees the star player of the Falcons, Eduardo López.

Everybody says Eduardo is the best ball player in the whole league. Everyone knows he is the best-looking guy at school. The girls all try to sit next to him at lunch. They try to talk to him in the hallway on the way to class.

All the girls do, except Carmen.

Once, Eduardo had laughed at her when she had dropped a high pop fly. The ball had gone foul just off third base. He stood and watched her as she followed the ball in the sky. Just as the ball was about to fall right into her glove, Eduardo let out a big burp. Carmen dropped the ball, and the whole team laughed.

The next day, he told everyone at school what had happened. Every time she walked by Eduardo and his friends, they would burp. That day seemed to last forever.

Even now, Carmen tries not to look at Eduardo. She doesn't want to give him another reason to laugh.

Carmen doesn't know why Eduardo doesn't like her. They have been playing in Little League together for the last three years. But Eduardo never speaks to her during the practices or the games.

Carmen has tried to be friendly. She even asked her mom for advice. Finally Carmen decided to ignore Eduardo right back.

So they hardly talked to each other all season. That is until this morning in homeroom.

If you were Carmen, would you want to be friends with Eduardo? Explain.

2 "You chicken?"

In homeroom that morning, Eduardo walked back and forth in the front of the classroom.

All the students sat in their seats and watched Eduardo strut.

"The Falcons are going to win. We're going to skunk the Cougars today," Eduardo said.

His pals all cheered and clapped.

Eduardo puffed up his chest and smiled. The smile filled his whole face.

A couple of the boys whistled.

When he said this, Carmen took a book and opened it in front of her face to hide. She hated the way Eduardo always acted so proud. She knew he was good, but did he have to spend every day telling the whole world? She sighed and slipped down in her seat.

Eduardo pointed to himself. "Yup. I'm going to hit another homerun today 'cause I'm the homerun king of the league."

She looked down at her book and kept her thoughts to herself. She didn't want to get into an argument with him.

Carmen groaned when Isidro Escobar stood up and coughed. "Excuse me," he said softly. No one else paid any attention to him.

"Eduardo, you're wrong," Isidro said as he pushed his glasses up his nose with his finger. All the boys around Eduardo became very quiet. They turned and looked at Isidro.

Eduardo walked down the aisle. His teammates moved out of the way. He stopped in front of Isidro. "What did you say?" Eduardo asked.

Isidro looked up at Eduardo. "I said you're wrong. You're not the homerun king."

"Oh, yeah? What do you know about it?" Eduardo asked.

"Well, according my records—and I've

watched every game—Carmen has hit more homeruns than you." Isidro looked back and pointed at Carmen. "Exactly one more."

Carmen wanted to disappear into the floor, but she sat up straight and stared at the two boys. She was very careful not to smile.

Eduardo looked at Carmen, then back to Isidro. "Oh, yeah? Is that what your records say?"

Isidro nodded. "They also say you have the highest batting average."

Carmen thought, Isidro wasn't the class brain for nothing.

Eduardo smiled and looked back at his buddies. All of them smiled back. Some of them stuck their thumbs up in the air.

Then Eduardo looked at Carmen. "So you think you're the homerun king?"

Isidro said, "Well, actually, since Carmen is a girl, she would be the homerun *queen.*" Eduardo turned back and glared at Isidro. If looks could kill, Isidro would have been bleeding all over the floor.

"No girl can be homerun king. Ever."

Eduardo moved around Isidro's desk to stand next to Carmen's.

Carmen didn't say anything. She looked back at him as hard as he looked at her.

"Today, I'm going to beat your record." Eduardo leaned across the desk and stuck a finger in Carmen's face. "And if I don't, I'll give you my glove. How's that?"

Everyone in the classroom gasped. Eduardo's glove was signed by Sammy Sosa.

Carmen shook her head. She didn't trust Eduardo.

Eduardo leaned closer. "You chicken?"

Carmen didn't move.

Eduardo was pointing his finger at Carmen again when the homeroom teacher walked in. "Mr. López, is there a problem here?" The homeroom teacher always called all the students by their last name.

Eduardo looked at Carmen, when he answered, "No, sir. We were just talking about the ball game this afternoon."

"Well, I'm sure everyone is very excited, but right now, we have to do our school work.

Everyone back to their seats, and let's begin."
The teacher clapped his hand three times.

As Eduardo moved away from Carmen, he whispered, "This afternoon, we'll find out who is the best." He walked back to his desk. He didn't look at Carmen again for the rest of the school day.

What's Eduardo's problem? Why is he acting this way?

3 The Last Inning

From the dugout, Carmen focuses her eyes on the game. She can still hear Eduardo's challenge echo in her head. "He's going to do it," she thinks. He hit two homers already. His team, the Falcons, has the lead. Meanwhile, Carmen is in a major-league slump. She struck out three times. "But if I could only get one more chance…," she thinks stubbornly.

Standing at the plate now is Raúl. He is a skinny boy with his hair cut short and a long pigtail down the back of his neck. He tugs at his helmet and swings his bat a couple of times to loosen up. He places one foot in the batter's box, then the other. The umpire calls, "Play ball!"

Raúl swings at the first ball.

"Strike," yells the umpire.

Everyone in the Cougar dugout moans. The ball was high. Carmen thinks that Raúl is just showing off. He shouldn't be swinging at dumb pitches. One more out and the game is over.

Raúl lets the next pitch go by. The umpire calls it a ball.

The count is one and one.

Carmen sees Raúl dig his toe into the dirt like the major league players on TV. This means he plans to hit the next ball really hard.

Raúl swings with all his might. The ball leaps off Raúl's bat and sails high over the shortstop's head. Raúl is safe on first.

Carmen's turn has come at last, but the coach calls her back. He sends Theo to the plate instead. She looks at the coach, but he's paying attention to the game.

Theo, short for Theodore, steps up to home plate. He is a lefty. The coach must be thinking the switch will upset the pitcher. Maybe Theo could draw a walk.

The pitcher throws the ball, and the umpire calls, "Ball one!"

Coach yells at Raúl to stay close to first base and to stop dancing around. Raúl grins at everyone in the dugout.

"Ball two."

The third pitch is also a ball. All Theo has to do is stand there and wait for ball four. Then he can walk to first base.

But the pitcher throws one right down the middle. So, Theo takes a swing. The ball flies past the pitcher's glove and rolls into the outfield for a single.

Raúl runs to second, and Theo makes it to first. Now there are two runners on base. The Cougars clap and whistle. They still have hope.

Carmen steps up to the plate again. Again, she hears the coach calling her name. She wants to pretend that she doesn't hear. But the coach calls her name a little bit louder this time. She sits back down. She holds the bat very tight in her hands, almost like she's choking it.

The coach sends Gilberto to bat. Gil is one of the team's best hitters. He's a big guy. And, he really knows how to put his weight behind the ball. But Gil is so slow. He can reach base only

if he can hit the ball far enough.

The Falcons' coach signals to his outfielders to play deep.

Gil is excited and swings at the very first pitch. The bat jumps out of his hands. It's a short hit to right field. The rightfielder can't get to it because he's standing too far back. He has to run to catch the ball on the first bounce. He throws the ball to first base. It's not a great throw.

Gil is running hard. Carmen sees Gil puffing all the way. He falls on the first base bag with a loud "Oooff!" His helmet flies off and rolls down the foul line. A big cloud of dust covers the air.

The Cougars cheer as Gil stands up. He is breathing hard. His face is sweaty and red. The umpire calls, "Safe!"

The bases are loaded. There are two outs.

The score is Falcons 8–Cougars 5.

The coach looks at Carmen and points to home plate. Carmen is finally up. "You can do it, slugger," he says.

How do you think Carmen feels now?

4 Carmen at Bat

Carmen walks up to the batter's box. On the way she stops and swings the bat a couple of times to warm up. The batting helmet is making her head itch. She can feel the sweat in her hair.

She doesn't look left or right, just straight ahead. She taps her cleats with the bat and steps into the batter's box.

Carmen hears her father yell, "Hit it out of the park!" Then her mother calls, "Do your best, honey. Just do your best."

Carmen smiles. Her parents are always like that. Her father wants her to go for it. Her mother says that doing your best is what counts. Her parents are great, but she needs quiet. She blocks out all the noise from the bleachers. She doesn't want to be daydreaming in the batter's box.

Carmen remembers how her father taught her to stare at the pitcher. He says that it makes pitchers worry. But Carmen doesn't think anything will make this pitcher worry.

Eduardo López leans forward. With one arm behind his back, he stares back at Carmen. It's not a friendly stare. He straightens up and pitches the ball.

The umpire yells, "Ball one."

The runners on base begin to shout, "C'mon on batter. Bring me home."

Carmen swings as the ball flies by.

The umpire calls, "Strike!"

Eduardo smiles. He turns around to look at the other ball players and yells, "Easy out." The rest of his team players chant, "Hey *battabattabatta*," trying to break her concentration.

The third pitch is high and outside.

The umpire calls, "Ball two."

Eduardo doesn't look worried. He holds up

his hand to his teammates. Again, they all start to chatter. Eduardo throws another pitch. It's low.

"Three balls and one strike."

Eduardo frowns. Everyone gets very quiet.

Carmen thinks about the next pitch. She says to herself, "If it's a ball, I walk to first base. The runner on third is forced home. That would give us one more run. But Eduardo won't allow that. He's proud. He'll go for the strike out to end the game."

Carmen's right. The pitch comes right down the middle, fast and hard. She swings too late. The umpire calls, "Strike two."

"Stop thinking!" Carmen tells herself. "You could have hit that one!"

It's a full count, three balls and two strikes.

This next ball is the one. "It's him or me," she thinks. She wipes a drop of sweat from her forehead and settles into her stance.

Eduardo fires another pitch right down the middle.

"Whack!" Everyone can hear the bat hit the ball. Carmen ignores all the cheering and clapping and speeds toward first base. The runners on the bases all take off. The centerfielder runs backwards. The ball is moving across the sky like a comet. He runs back nearly to the fence.

Suddenly a breeze pushes the ball to the left. The centerfielder moves under it with his eyes glued upward. Meanwhile, the leftfielder is moving toward the ball, too. Just as the ball is about to come down, the outfielders crash. They fall to the ground in a heap of arms and legs. Plop. The ball hits the grass and rolls away.

Carmen blazes past first. The coach waves at the other boys to keep running. Carmen is right behind Gil, yelling at him to run faster. Gil huffs and puffs his way to second.

Raúl cruises from third base to home plate.

In the outfield, the players get up. They're dazed but not hurt. Right away, they start arguing about who was at fault.

Theo streaks by third base and races home.

"Faster!" Carmen yells to Gil as he heads for third. Gil's head wobbles like an overgrown tomato.

Out in the field, Eduardo is screaming,

"Throw the ball! One of you just throw the ball!"

The leftfielder throws it in. The shortstop jumps up to make the catch. He turns around and throws the ball to the catcher. Gil is headed for home to score the tying run.

Everyone in the bleachers—moms and dads for both teams—are on their feet.

"Come on, Gil!" Carmen screams. "I'm right behind you!"

Gil puts his head down and begins to grunt. The catcher has the ball. He's defending home plate. "Oh, no!" Carmen thinks. "That's it! Game over." Suddenly, Gil takes a deep breath of air and roars, "Ahhhhh!" Waving his hands over his head, he runs for home plate.

Carmen sees the catcher's eyes go round and big. Gil is running straight at him. The catcher steps back in fear. The baseball skips out of his mitt and drops to the ground. Gil lands on home plate with both feet. Everyone can hear the thud.

The umpire cries, "You're safe!"

Carmen is running at full speed, heading for home. The catcher picks up the ball. She stops and turns back toward third.

Eduardo yells, "Throw me the ball! Throw me the ball!"

Eduardo has gotten behind Carmen. He's blocking her way back to third base. The catcher throws the ball to Eduardo.

Carmen is in a pickle.

She runs toward home plate again. Eduardo throws the ball to the catcher.

So, she turns around and runs back to third base.

The ball flies over her head into Eduardo's mitt. He holds it up so she can see it.

They are standing closer to home plate than they are to third base. Eduardo comes after her. He wants to be the one to tag her out.

Carmen's heart hits against her ribs hard. She can't hear anyone or anything. All she can see is Eduardo's face and the ball in his hand. She looks at Eduardo and smiles.

"It's pay-back time, Eduardo," she thinks. She swallows down a big gulp of air. "BURP!" Eduardo is so surprised that for a moment he just stands there with his mouth hanging open and the ball in his hand. Carmen takes off and heads for home. Eduardo throws the ball hard and fast, just like when he pitches.

"Bap!" the fastball smacks into Carmen's helmet. The ball bounces off her head and goes into the air. Carmen stumbles to home plate. All of a sudden her face hits the dust and the world turns black.

How did Carmen keep from getting tagged out?

5 Game Over

Carmen would never again laugh at cartoon characters who get hit in the head. Those birds chirping and flying around their heads weren't so funny anymore. She could hear them, too.

Finally Carmen opens her eyes. Her mother is right there.

Her mother leans over and whispers, "What's your name, honey?"

"Mom," Carmen said. "I'm your daughter. You should know that my name is Carmen."

With those words, the crowd standing around Carmen shouted with joy, "She's all right!"

Carmen saw Eduardo let out a breath in relief. She had been out cold for almost a minute.

The umpire stands and yells, "She's safe."

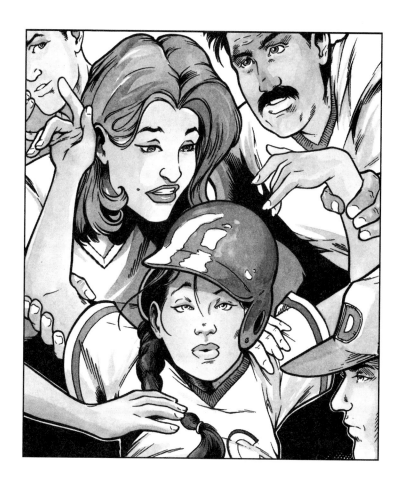

Everybody from the Cougars dugout jumps up and down and throws their gloves in the air.

"Carmen!" Gil shouts, "You scored the winning run!"

Isidro jumps up with his notebook in his hand. "That counts as an in-the-park homer.

Carmen and Eduardo are both homerun kings. I mean, king and queen!"

Carmen's dad lifts her up and carries her off the field. She says, "Dad, I want to walk. I don't want the boys to think I'm a wimp." But her dad carries her all the way to the bleachers.

One of the grandmothers gives her a cold pack to put on her head. Grandmothers are great. They carry safety pins, if your uniform rips. They have baby wipes to clean your face. They also have plenty of bandages and the stuff that stings, if you scrape yourself sliding into base.

Her parents make Carmen sit quietly while all her teammates shake hands with the other team.

Eduardo comes over to where Carmen is sitting on the bleachers. Her father stands up and puts on an angry face. Carmen isn't worried. She has seen that face on her father before. It's his 'I'm-protecting-my-daughter,' angry face. He stares down at Eduardo. Carmen's mom pulls her father away. They stand on the other side of her.

Eduardo sticks out his hand. "Good game, Carmen. I'm sorry about hitting you. I didn't mean to. Honest."

Carmen shakes hands with him. "I know you didn't mean to hit me. You couldn't help it. You don't have enough control," she says smiling.

Eduardo looks at his feet, then reaches out with his glove in his hand. "Well, I didn't get more homeruns than you, Carmen. So I guess this is yours."

Carmen looks at the glove, then at her father. Her father shrugs. He is letting her decide.

She takes the glove.

A real big league glove, she thinks. She can feel how heavy it is in her hand and imagines playing in Cougar Stadium or Fenway Park.

Carmen smiles. "It doesn't fit me yet," she says. She hands the glove back to Eduardo. "But next year, when I win the glove again, I'm keeping it."

Do you think Carmen and Eduardo might become friends? Why or why not?

Meet the Author

I didn't always know that I was going to be a writer. But I always liked to write. In high school, I wrote a 25-page ending to a story and received an "F" because I misspelled so many words. I was 33 when I took my first writing class in college and realized that I had talent (even if I couldn't spell).

When you're young, there's a sense of not knowing who you are or what you are. You doubt yourself. There's a lot of pressure from the outside. You worry: Am I enough? Do I act like everyone else? Will I ever be able to learn like everyone else?

I want you to know that you're enough just as you are. What's important is to show up each day despite these doubts. Put one foot in front of the other, one word after the other. Sometimes that effort takes more courage than anything else.

—*Jo Ann Yolanda Hernández*